Rookie reader®

Baby
in the
House

By David F. Marx

Illustrated by Cynthia Fisher

Children's Press®
A Division of Grolier Publishing
New York • London • Hong Kong • ~~Sydney~~

For the Chiba family, best of friends
—C.F.

Reading Consultants
Linda Cornwell
Coordinator of School Quality and Professional Improvement
(Indiana State Teachers Association)

Katharine A. Kane
Education Consultant
(Retired, San Diego County Office of Education
and San Diego State University)

Visit Children's Press® on the Internet at:
http://publishing.grolier.com

Library of Congress Cataloging-in-Publication Data
Marx, David F.
    Baby in the house / by David F. Marx; illustrated by Cynthia Fisher.
      p . cm. — (Rookie reader)
    Summary: Eve is not sure how she feels when a new baby arrives in the house, but
she soon learns that being a sister can be fun.
    ISBN 0-516-21688-0 (lib. bdg.)   0-516-27045-1 (pbk.)
    [1. Babies Fiction. 2. Brothers and sisters Fiction.] I. Fisher, Cynthia, ill. II. Title.
III. Series.
PZ7.M36822Bab 2000
[E] — dc 21   99-15866
                                                                        CIP

GROLIER
PUBLISHING   1 2 3 4 5 6 7 8 9 10 R 09 08 07 06 05 04 03 02 01 00

A baby is in the house,
and Eve is not happy.

The baby grabs too much.

The baby smells too much.

The baby costs too much.

The baby cries too much.

11

A baby is in the house,
and Eve is looking closer.

The baby laughs a lot.

16

The baby smells sweet.

The baby looks cute
in his new snowsuit.

A baby is in the house, and Eve is playing with him.

The baby has great toys.

The baby reads Eve's books

The baby pats Eve's face.

The baby holds on tight,

but Eve loves the baby.

A baby is in the house, and Eve is happy.

Word List (42 words)

a	happy	new
and	has	not
baby	him	on
books	his	pats
but	holds	playing
closer	house	reads
costs	in	smells
cries	is	snowsuit
cute	laughs	sweet
Eve	looking	the
Eve's	looks	tight
face	lot	too
grabs	loves	toys
great	much	with

About the Author

David F. Marx is a children's author and editor who lives in Newtown, Connecticut.

About the Illustrator

Cynthia Fisher has built her career as an illustrator over the past ten years. She has illustrated a variety of books, including pop-ups, easy readers, middle-grade readers, and picture books. She lives in Buckland, Massachusetts, with her husband, Marcus, and children, Kiera and Rory.